Call My Name

Robin Rance

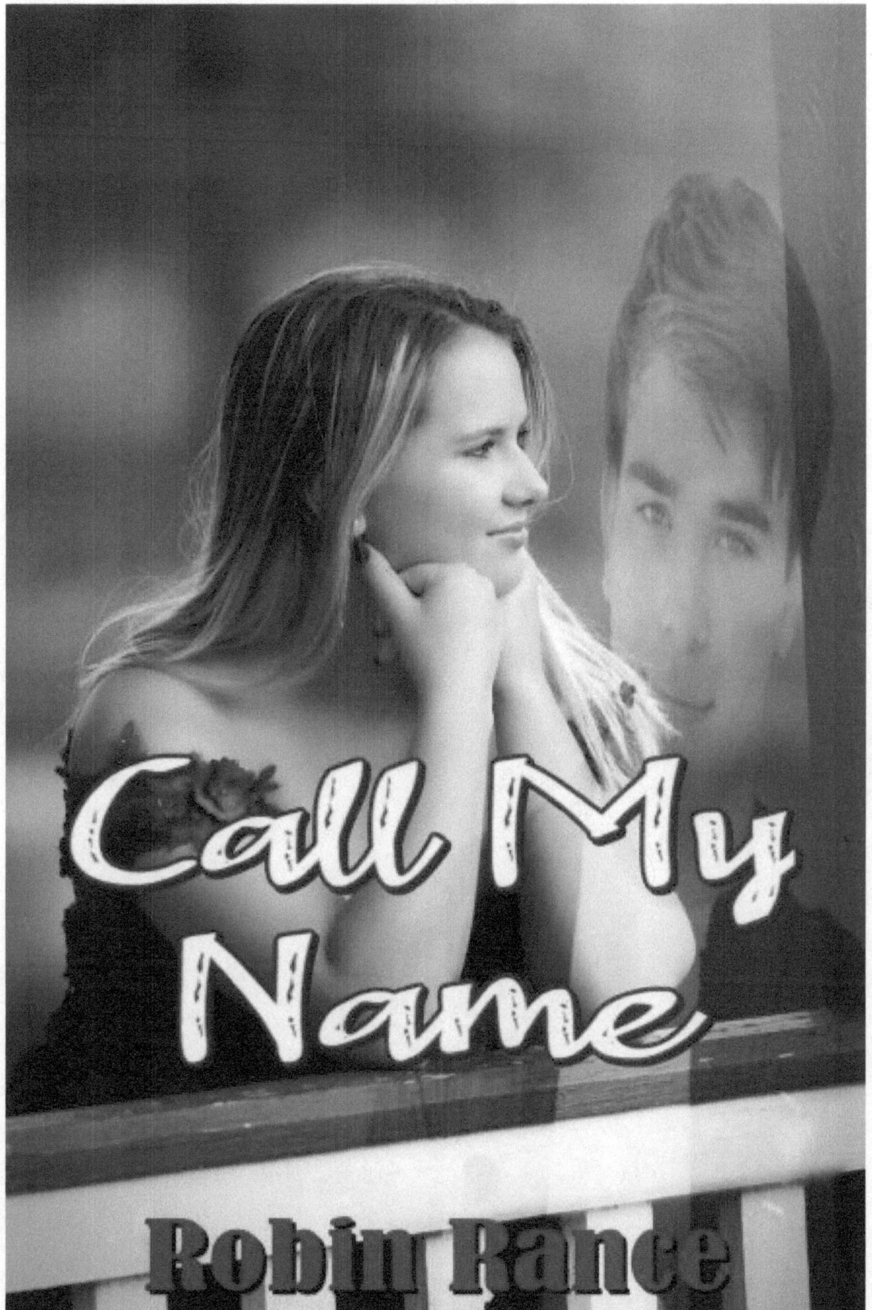
Call My
Name
Robin Rance

Call My Name

Ruby **Lane** is a typical girl of seventeen, who is crazy for boys, clothes, and friends, and though she may not act like it, she wants to do what's best for her family.

She continually does whatever she can at church to raise the eyebrows of the elders.

She's crushing on a boy her mother doesn't approve of, and does everything she can to change her mother's mind about him.

But then she meets Kyle.

Kyle has the kindest eyes of anyone she's ever met. But when Ruby tries to talk to him, she learns he's deaf, autistic, and brilliant.

But after he's teased at school for the way he talks, Kyle won't say her name.

Ruby would do almost anything to hear him speak her name out loud.

Dedication:

This story is for anyone who's crushed on another person.

It's a sweet story of a girl's first real love and the lengths she will go to for him to notice her.

Copyright Notice

Chapter One

Church Social

IT'S NOT VERY OFTEN that I come across someone who takes my breath away at first sight. Not since the first time that I looked into Kyle's eyes.

It happened again, just a few minutes ago. I brushed past him, walking through the airport as I was leaving after dropping my daughter off to catch a flight. I stopped where I stood and followed his movements as he hurried to his next destination.

I knew I'd never see him again but continued to watch until he was no longer visible...

"MOM, COULD YOU PLEASE fix my zipper, it won't stay up!"

"Then change your dress, for heaven's sake, Ruby. I don't always have time to do your bidding. I've got to finish these pies for the church picnic, or Maggie Simpleton will jump in and offer hers the next time, and I swear she does it all for the attention. Do you know she even..."?

I stood there as my mom babbled on trying to fix the zipper myself. This was the dress that Noah said brought out the dark blue specs in my eyes. I had to wear it to the picnic, so he'd stay focused on me.

"Did you hear what I just said? I swear, Ruby if it weren't for that boy you're obsessing over, things would get done around here much quicker." I watched as my mother grabbed a dishtowel from the top of the cupboard.

She used it to wipe off her hands. "Turn around; maybe it's just stuck in the binding." I felt her jiggle the zipper and at the same time, push on the two sides of my dress. Then I heard her sigh, and felt the zipper close as she pulled it up to the top.

"Thanks, Mom. I'll help you finish packing up the pies in the boxes, just give me a minute to slip my pantyhose on." I leaned in and kissed her on the cheek.

"I sure hope that you made Noah's favorite kind?"

She shook her head back and forth at me and made that tsking noise she made in the back of her throat when she was annoyed. "Ruby, you need to slow down. You're only seventeen; that's much too young to be involved with someone. Besides that, isn't he too old for you?"

“Which of the pies do you want to keep together?" I turned around and picked up the pile of flat boxes and began laying them out on the kitchen table to put each of the pastries into; it would make it much easier to carry them all.

"You know, Noah just turned eighteen. He's barely four months older than I am."

My mother walked over and rearranged the pies into groups of four. "Keep all the fruit ones together; I think there are enough cream ones to fill two of the boxes. And yes, I made a few of the cherry cheese pies so Noah could have more than one helping. I put them on the top shelf in the fridge to start setting up. Are his parents going to be there today?"

"I think his mother is, his dad is off on some business trip again. Poor Noah, I know he's trying to keep it quiet, but I think his mom and dad are having marital trouble. He said his dad has been taking longer business trips. Between you and me, I don't think they're business trips at all. Noah told me when his dad gets home, it's usually late, and he smells like a brewery."

"Ruby Lane, how would that boy know what a brewery smells like?" Mom stopped what she was doing and stared off into space. Perhaps she was contemplating what I'd just said.

"Once you've completed with that task, why don't you finish getting dressed. I'll have you whip up the cream for me when you're ready. Ruby, I hope your father remembered to get me more sugar."

WE MADE IT TO THE PICNIC with all eighteen pies in tow: not one mishap.

One of the elders was standing outside and hurried out to the car to help us bring them inside. "Mrs. Johnson, the wind is picking up outside, so we decided to have the picnic inside the church. Let me help you get this into the kitchen."

"Careful with them, Elder Smith. Most of them can go inside and be left on the tables. However, the cream ones need to go into the refrigerator. I marked them with a red crayon.

"Ruby, take the whipped cream and set it inside the big fridge; we can separate it into smaller bowls when it's time for dessert." Mom grabbed one of the boxes containing her precious cream pies and followed me into the kitchen.

"When is Dad supposed to be here?" I opened the fridge and helped my mom take the pies out of the box and set them carefully inside the refrigerator along with the whipped cream.

"He's stopping at the new neighbors' house to give them a ride here. I hope they come this time. He's been trying to get them to go to church with us on Sunday. So far, only the youngest boy, Kevin, has come. I think they have a daughter who is thirteen or fourteen, the little boy

Kevin is eleven, and they have one more son who just turned seventeen." She counted her pies one more time and then shut the door.

"Mrs. Deegan is a sweet woman; however, she's very shy. I think she'd love it here. Your father hasn't met her husband yet. He always goes into his bedroom whenever your father stops by for a visit."

"It would be nice if he was here helping you carry all these pies inside. I'm just saying..." My parents meant well, but not everyone wanted to be converted to the church. "Sometimes the way they do things around here is kind of screwy if you ask me."

Really screwy.

"My goodness, where did that come from? Ruby Lane don't let Bishop Arnett hear you say that. Let's hurry to the church hall and see if they could use our help setting the tables."

I followed my mom into the large room. There were already kids running around unattended, their parents oblivious to the destruction they caused. I did my best to ignore what they were doing, and searched for Noah's family. I didn't see them yet.

I turned around and ran smack dab into the middle of Bishop Arnett. "Sorry, Bishop."

He steadied me then smiled. "That's quite alright, Ruby. It's been a few months since we've chatted, would you make an appointment with Elder Evans to come and talk to me soon?" Suddenly his tone changed, "Is your dad here yet?"

"No, Bishop. He stopped over to see if the new family wanted to come to the picnic, he should be here soon." I knew what he wanted to ask me, but I didn't want a job in the church. The last time I was asked to serve was in the nursery. I was stuck there for three years.

"I've got a question for you, Bishop."

"What is it, Ruby?"

My mother wasn't anywhere near, so I decided to question him about some of the strange habits the church had. "Bishop, my mom thinks I'm just impertinent, but I wondered...if we are all supposed to be a family, then why is it that my mom and dad never come to church together. He's always off helping other families, and she's off doing her thing as well. I know it sounds kind of selfish, but we never go to any church functions like a family. Isn't that the point?"

"Well Ruby," The bishop was close to thirty years older than me. I was sure that when he was my age, he must have been a knockout. He had the best smile. "I must get this picnic started, we will talk about it when you meet with me."

He turned around to leave, but then spun around, "Would you like to say the opening prayer and offer a blessing on the food?"

"Not really." Now came my penance for being impolite, or as my mother called, it, impertinent.

"I knew I could count on you. Ruby, I'll see you inside the chapel."

Chapter Two

The Prayer

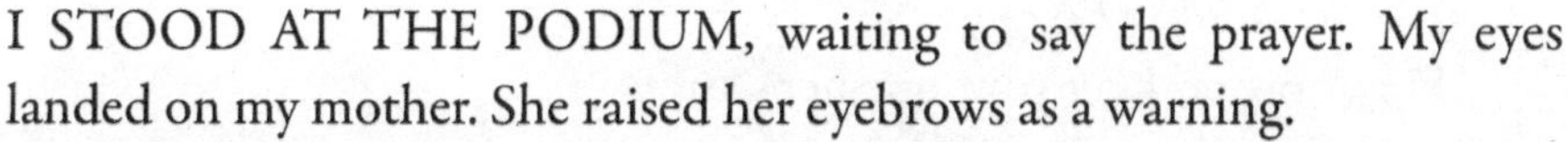

I STOOD AT THE PODIUM, waiting to say the prayer. My eyes landed on my mother. She raised her eyebrows as a warning.

My father had finally shown up to the indoor picnic with his guests. He had Kevin, Mrs. Deegan, and her oldest son with him. It was a good thing that Mother had saved a place for five just in case. And from the looks of Mrs. Deegan's hair, the wind must have kicked up quite a bit. I bit down on my bottom lip to stop from giggling, but stopped after the warning look my mother gave me.

How did she always manage to know what I was thinking?

The room was full of people, and they were restless and tired of waiting. I hated saying the prayer, and I thought about drawing out the blessing on the food just a little longer than was necessary to have some fun. What would happen if I misbehaved. My parents would both yell at me later, that's what would happen.

Oh well.

I waited for everyone to take their seats, and then the room got quiet. I began, "Our dear father in heaven..." Once I was finished, I left the podium and rushed to meet my family.

My father stood and smiled, "Thank you, Ruby, that was very nice."

Well, at least I had my father's approval. "Thanks, Dad" I looked for the place that I asked my brother to save for me, and somebody else was sitting in my seat. Now I was stuck next to Kevin, and his older brother sat on the other side of him. We hadn't met yet. He didn't even look in my direction when I was seated, and for some reason, that really bugged me.

Probably because I was mad that hadn't seen Noah yet.

"Hey, Kevin, what's your brother's name?" I looked straight at him when I asked; he still didn't look at me.

"It's Kyle, and he's deaf. Are they bringing our food to us?"

Deaf?

"No, they will excuse each table one at a time, we're lucky we're not the last one" Now I was obsessed with Kyle.

What color were his eyes?

"Hey, how do I get your brother's attention?"

"Well, he's also autistic. He loves colors and anything shiny; that will always get his attention. Do you have anything like that?"

I did. I had a necklace with a broken clasp. Noah had given to me, but I couldn't wear it anyway because I didn't want my mom to see it. I fished it out of my pocket and held it out in front of me.

It started spinning in the slight breeze and caught Kyle's interest. He watched it spin, and then he looked directly at me.

At that moment, time stood still. He had the kindest eyes that I had ever seen. I caught my breath before smiling at him."

"Hey Ruby, now you can just wave at him. I told him your name." It seemed rather silly, but I did as Kevin showed me to do.

Kyle returned my gesture, and then signed, "How are you?"

Talk about having nothing to say.

Now I wished I had taken more sign language. I could only mouth the words back to him, "I am fine, how are you?" His smile was huge.

I turned my head away from him and stared at the empty table in front of me.

What's wrong with me?

Now I was all tongue-tied, and he couldn't even hear me if I had spoken. So, I continued to stare at my twiddling thumbs, not sure what to do next.

Kevin whispered, "Do you want to help Kyle get his food? I think they're signaling for our table to go up next?" Kevin stood up, and Kyle moved over onto the seat next to me. He smiled, and continued to watch me.

I stared back as I called out to his brother, "Kevin, wait, what do I do next."

Kyle leaned closer to me and wrinkled up his nose. In a nasal voice that I'd heard other deaf people use, he said, "Put a chain awound my neck and poo me behind you wike a dok."

"What?" At first, I didn't know he was kidding and just stared at him; I was horrified by what he'd said.

He chuckled, but then stood up and took my hand. I set my necklace on the chair and let him lead me to the beginning of the food line.

Chapter Three

He Doesn't Forget

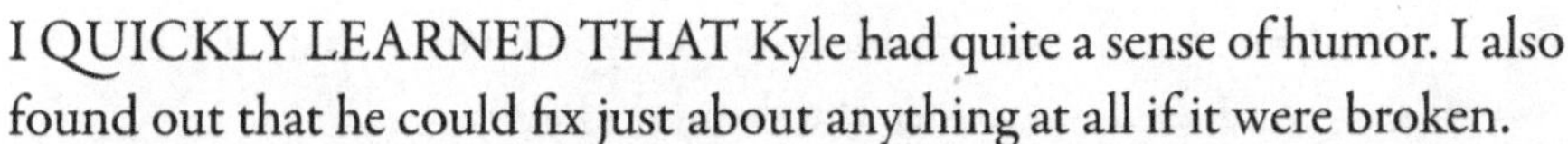

I QUICKLY LEARNED THAT Kyle had quite a sense of humor. I also found out that he could fix just about anything at all if it were broken.

Soon after the church picnic, he returned my necklace to me with the clasp fixed. I also discovered that he could read lips. I had to be very careful around him when I spoke.

"Thank you, Kyle."

"Welcome, Oobie."

And that was the thing that bothered me the most about Kyle. It was a silly thing, really, but I wanted him to say my name the right way. But how would that ever happen? When I got a chance, I'd ask his brother, Kevin. Maybe he could give me some ideas.

THE DEEGAN FAMILY CONTINUED to go to church, and I looked forward to seeing him, and them every week. Soon after that, Kyle started going to the same school that I did.

He was enrolled in all the classes for special needs kids. I only saw him briefly in the halls, but he always got excited when he saw me, and called my name to get my attention.

It was okay until the first time Noah met me in the hall for lunch. Noah was there with some of his jock friends, and I tried to hide my face as soon as I saw Kyle walking toward me through the school hall.

"Oobie, hey, Oobie."

Noah's friends saw me ducking, and started mimicking the way Kyle spoke. "Oobie doobie doo. Want a Scoobie snack, Oobie."

"Knock it off, you big jerks! Why are your friends always so mean, Noah Smith? Tell them to stop what they're doing, or I'm going to..."

"You're going to do what, Ruby? They're just having a little fun with him."

"But it's wrong. He can't help it if he's deaf and dumb. Tell them to leave him alone. He doesn't know how to say my name, that's all."

"Guys, you heard her. Leave the dumb kid alone."

"He's deaf, but thanks, Noah."

"MOM, I DON'T WANT TO go to church today. Please let me stay home."

"Why, Ruby? Is it because you have that interview with Bishop Arnett? You can't avoid him forever, you know."

"Yes, I know that, but I'm sure he's going to ask me to help do something at church. What's wrong with taking some time off. I know, Mom, don't tell me. It's a calling from God. But why is it always me that gets asked?

"You aren't the only one, and you know it."

"I know. I'll probably get stuck in the nursery again." I loved the kids, but I I wanted to go to class with my friends.

And Kyle.

"It could be worse, you know. You could be teaching a class for all of the know-it-all senior women. The only thing that's gone my way lately is that most of the ones who sit up front now, do it because they can't hear me. They're afraid to say anything because they're not sure they heard it correctly. It can be entertaining sometimes. It's like a weekly game of secret." Mom started giggling, which quickly spread to me, and before long, we both had tears rolling down out cheeks.

She pulled the tissue from her bra, and wiped her cheeks. "Go and get yourself dressed. Why don't you wear that pretty dark blue dress that Nana gave you? I'm sure once you're there, you'll be glad you came."

"Fine, but after church, I'm coming straight home. I'm tired of doing service projects."

"Ruby,"

"I'm just saying..."

SURE ENOUGH, AS SOON as we stepped inside the church, the bishop was there waiting for me. "Ruby Lane, since you're a few minutes early, would you like to speak with me before church begins?"

I glanced at my mother. "Sure, Bishop. Save me a place, Mom."

It went just as I had expected, but the Bishop threw in an added distraction. I would be working in the nursery with Pamela Jennings. And just for kicks and giggles, he was going to ask Kyle Deegan to also help with the class. There was a small boy in that class who was deaf. He figured since Kyle was new, it would help him find his role in the church quicker, and at the same time, he knowing sign language, would make things easier for us, and the kid.

My mom took my hand and pulled me into the bench to sit by her. "Ruby, I'm so proud of you. I can't wait to hear what you'll be doing. The services are ready to start; we can talk afterward."

Right after the opening prayer, my father showed up with the Deegan family. All of them except the father. I wondered if we would ever meet him. We all scooted down to make room for the family to sit.

Right away, I smiled at Kyle, but he turned his head.

How did he not see me?

I'd look for him after church, and tell him about the bishop's plans. At least I'd have a friendly face working with me in the nursery. We were to start next week; things moved quickly in church.

Bishop Arnett stood outside of the chapel doors and shook everyone's hands as they exited the room. His smile was meant to put you at ease.

I knew better.

"Ruby, thanks again for agreeing to help."

"As if I had any choice."

"Ruby Lane, watch your manners. Bishop, the services were very uplifting and inspiring. I needed to hear your message today; it will put me in the right spirit to teach my class." She subtly, but firmly took my arm, "Ruby, I will see you after the rest of the meetings. Behave yourself."

"Gotcha."

Mom reached for my father's hand, and he leaned in a gave her a quick kiss before they went their separate ways inside the building.

I was left alone with Kyle. We hadn't spoken at school at all this week. I hadn't even seen him in the halls before lunch: not since Noah's friends had teased him.

I peeked at him; I hoped to see his smile. His eyes when he saw me in the halls at school always lit up. But today they seemed to have lost some of their spark. He also appeared to be avoiding me.

Could that be true?

I put my hand out and touched his arm; it was a few seconds before he looked at me. "Kyle, I guess we will be working together in the nursery starting next week. I can't wait to have you there." Nothing, not a word.

"How are things going at school, I haven't seen you at all in the last few days?"

Kyle usually spoke as he signed. This time, when he answered me, it was only with his signing. Once again, I wished that I had learned more sign language.

"I'm not sure what you are trying to tell me, Kyle. Can you say it out loud, or at least mouth the words for me?"

He stared at me for a few seconds, then turned and walked away.

"Fine, then don't talk to me. Geez." The only thing that made me feel better as I watched him walking away was knowing we would be spending a lot more time together in church. I didn't see him at school, but he wouldn't be able to avoid me here.

Just you wait.

AFTER THE MEETINGS were over, I found my mom gathering her visual tools and the other books and scriptures that she'd used for her lesson. "Can we go home now?"

"Your father left earlier to take Mrs. Arnett home. She wasn't feeling very well. Kyle went home with her. We're going to drop Kevin off at home, on our way to ours. Ruby, help me finish straightening up the room."

She leaned in closer and whispered. "The old biddies don't know how to keep still. Look at this room; everything was lined up in neat rows when I first got here, and now..." She waved at one of the older ladies as she left the room. "For a while, I thought they were playing musical chairs. How was your day?"

"Okay, I guess." I helped her put her teaching tools into the trunk of the car. I climbed into the back seat, and Kevin got in next to me.

"What's up with your brother, Kyle? He didn't want to talk to me at all today. Is he sick or something?"

"He doesn't forget."

That puzzled me. "What do you mean by that? Forget what?"

"At school last week, he said you called him dumb. Kyle doesn't forget those things."

"I never called him dumb. I don't know what you are talking about."

Kevin looked straight at me. "I heard him telling my mother the story; he doesn't lie either, Ruby. He told her that he called your name, and you told the boys around you that he was deaf and dumb. He isn't dumb, Ruby."

"I know he isn't. Did I really say that? If I did, I don't remember...oh, crap. I didn't mean it. Honestly, I didn't."

"Well Kyle doesn't know that. He doesn't forget, Ruby."

We pulled up in front of the Deegan's home, and Kevin jumped out. I saw Kyle peek out his bedroom window. I should have asked my mother to stop the car for a minute and let me go inside to apologize to him. But I didn't.

Chapter Four

Sign language

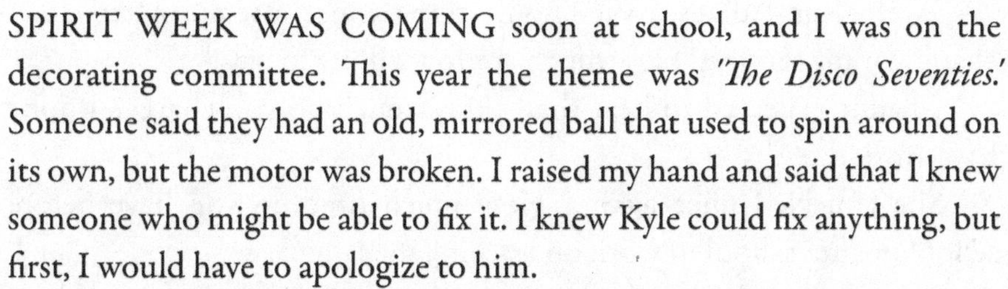

SPIRIT WEEK WAS COMING soon at school, and I was on the decorating committee. This year the theme was *'The Disco Seventies.'* Someone said they had an old, mirrored ball that used to spin around on its own, but the motor was broken. I raised my hand and said that I knew someone who might be able to fix it. I knew Kyle could fix anything, but first, I would have to apologize to him.

We had six weeks to come up with the decorations and to get the disco ball rolling again. That meant I had my work cut out for me.

I still hadn't seen Kyle in the halls at school, and I wanted to talk to him before we began working together in the nursery at church. It would be uncomfortable for everyone if I didn't tell him what had happened. But how would I do that?

I did have another idea that I was working on. Hopefully, if everything went the way I hoped it would, we would be friends again. I didn't tell anyone in my family what I was doing, but I was determined to succeed.

After school was over, I hurried into Miss Branson's room. She was one of the special needs teachers, and she also taught sign language. "Miss Branson, I want to learn sign language. How long does that take?"

Miss Branson was one of the prettiest teachers in the school. She had curly blonde hair and the bluest eyes I had ever seen on a grown woman.

She looked at me with those blue eyes and smiled. "You are Ruby, right?"

"Yes, Ruby Lane Johnson. Does it take a long time to learn sign language?"

She chuckled. "That all depends. What are you learning it for, how much time do you have to devote to it, and who will be teaching it to you?"

"I was hoping to learn it from you." I decided it wouldn't hurt to tell a little fib. "I'm going to be working in the nursery at church; there is a boy who will be there with me who is deaf. I want to be able to communicate with him."

"Well, Ruby, that's a very noble thing you're attempting to do. I charge for my services. How much are you willing to pay?"

I hadn't expected to hear that. "How much do you charge? I don't have any money."

She chuckled once again. "How much time do you have before school or after school to work on learning the language?"

"I can come at least an hour before school and stay an hour afterward as well. Will that be enough time to learn it in say, six weeks?"

"That depends, Ruby. If you come every day and spend two hours here with me, then you might be able to pull it off, it also depends on how quickly you can pick it up. But you must also earn my services."

I watched Miss Branson turn around and start gathering her supplies and stacking them in neat piles on the long table against the wall. So I hurried over to the table and started helping her.

"Miss Branson, I really need to learn the language, so tell me what I have to do."

"You can come every morning before school for an hour and help me prepare my lessons for the day. If we get done quicker then we will have more time to work on your signing skills. The last hour of the day is all yours unless I have a staff meeting or something else comes up. Those are my terms. You can think about it for a few days if you would like."

I stopped what I was doing to think. I thought about my daily activities. They weren't too important, but I did have a few chores to help with now and then before I went to school. With the disco ball coming, I'd have after-school activities to attend to as well.

So for me to do as miss Branson asked, I'd have to get up an hour earlier every day, plus I'd have to get to bed sooner. It would be tough at first, but it was a small price to pay for what I would get out of it.

I stuck my hand out in front of me. "Miss Branson, it's a deal. I'll see you at six tomorrow morning."

She smiled, and instead of shaking my hand, she signed and spoke the words, "Welcome, Ruby."

"Good Morning, Ruby." She mouthed the words along with signing. It was early Thursday, and now every morning when I greeted Miss Branson, I signed the words back to her before I helped her organize for the day.

MISS BRANSON TOLD ME she would start with the basics, family, mom, dad, and we would practice those words until I had them down.

"Ruby, I'm very pleased with your progress. You are very adept at picking things up." Miss Branson smiled and then started separating papers into piles on her desktop.

"Really? Yay. I can't wait to put sentences together. How long do you think it will be before I'm able to do that?"

"It depends. If you had someone whom you could practice with, you might learn faster. Do you know someone who knows sign language?"

I did, but the reason I was learning it was to surprise him. Then I remembered someone else who might help me. "I might, but it's going to cost me."

"It's your choice, Ruby. How much are you willing to do to learn this language?"

She was right, it was up to me. I was desperate to learn it, no matter what I had to do. I'd ask Kevin if he would be willing to help me when I saw him at church on Sunday. Maybe we could trade services. I knew he was struggling in math. I'd offer him my math skills he'd help me learn sign language.

I left Miss Branson's class a few minutes early every day. I knew that was Kyle's first class, and I didn't want to accidentally run into him. I still looked for him every day in the halls around lunchtime. I hadn't seen him at all since that afternoon when Noah and his friends had made fun of him.

Stupid me should have done something more to apologize to him then. If I had, maybe we would still be communicating. And still, be friends.

I was running late this morning; I had forgotten my book and hurried back to my locker to get it before I went to my geography class. I came around the corner and saw, Noah with a girl that I didn't care for at all.

Sheila Long wasn't a nice person. She was stuck up, she was a gossip and a trouble maker. They were holding hands in front of his first-period class. I saw him before he noticed me, but I must have gasped out loud when I turned to leave.

He dropped her hand, then called for me to stop. "Ruby, it's not what you think. Come back."

"Right." I didn't need the book that bad, nor did I need to see Sheila's smug face. She'd been after Noah ever since she learned he was interested in me.

I continued blindly down the hall and almost ran into the classroom.

My friend, Deborah, smiled at me, but then her look changed quickly into one of concern. "Ruby, what's wrong?"

I choked out the words, "Deb, I can't talk about it right now; class is about to start."

I sat down at my desk next to hers, and she reached over and squeezed my hand. "It's Noah, isn't it? I wanted to tell you about him and Sheila, but I didn't have the heart. I'm sorry, Ruby."

"You knew?"

The bell rang, and the classroom grew quiet. Mr. Christiansen was a stickler for the rules, and if he caught, Deborah and me chatting, he'd stick me between someone else.

I mouthed the words, *'Talk later,'* before I focused on him.

The class went horribly long. I got docked for not having my book with me, and I was called up in front of the classroom to draw a map on the chalkboard with one of Noah's friends, Matthew. He was the one who had instigated the teasing of Kyle the week before.

He whispered to me just before we started drawing, "How's Oobie doo?"

I told Matthew to shut his mouth, and Mr. Christiansen heard me. He told me to come to his class after school to help him correct papers and to work on my anger.

That made me even angrier, and it meant that I would miss going to Miss Branson's class. I was already in trouble, so I mouthed back, *'You're an ass.'*

The entire front row witnessed it, and for the rest of the day, I was teased. I wanted to go home early, but I couldn't because of what happened. Deborah saw the kind of mood I was in, and she also avoided me for the rest of the day.

AFTER I FINISHED LUNCH, I hurried to Miss Branson's classroom. I wanted to let her know that I wouldn't make it after school; I didn't want her to think I wasn't interested in coming.

I knocked before I entered her class and saw Kyle and her talking together in sign language. I studied them for a few minutes before Kyle realized I was in the room. He turned beet red, and then he looked back at Miss Branson and signed something quickly. She shook her head at him and smiled.

He went to move past me, and I reached out and took his arm to stop him. I did know how to sign hello, and I wanted to show him. "Hello, Kyle. Did you have lunch?" He smiled at me then shook his head no. He hurried past me and almost ran out the door.

Miss Branson asked from behind me, "Did you need something, Ruby?"

I sighed loudly, and she chuckled. "I wish I could read minds sometimes."

"Ruby, I can't help you with that one. Did you need something else?"

"Yes, I got in trouble in my first-period class. I've been ordered to go there after school and help Mr. Christiansen correct papers in his classroom. I just didn't want you thinking I was blowing you off."

"Thanks for letting me know, Ruby. I've got another student who needs my help with a problem that he's having, so that works out well.

"Will I see you tomorrow morning?"

"Absolutely, Miss Branson."

Chapter Five

Upper Hand

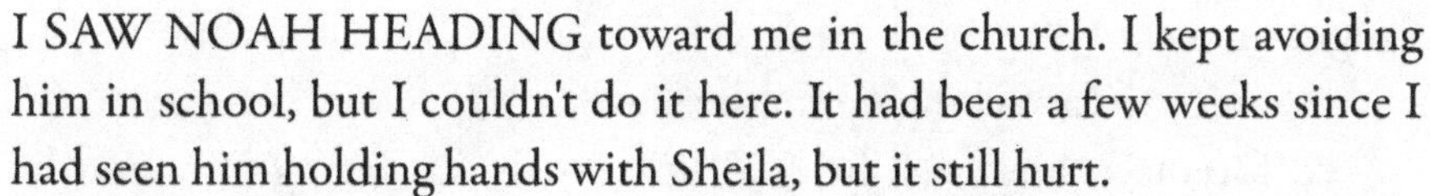

I SAW NOAH HEADING toward me in the church. I kept avoiding him in school, but I couldn't do it here. It had been a few weeks since I had seen him holding hands with Sheila, but it still hurt.

"Ruby, I'm sorry. You're not still mad at me, are you? It was nothing, Sheila is just a friend."

"I have other male friends beside you, Noah. I don't hold their hands and gaze soulfully into their eyes in a dark hallway."

"Soulfully, what's that supposed to mean, Ruby?"

"It means I don't want any part of your stupid games. I've moved on, and I suggest you do the same." I bit the inside of my lip to stop it from trembling. When I was upset I usually chook all over.

He shook his head back and forth, "Then it's true, you have a thing for the retarded kid, don't you?"

I don't know where I got the strength or the courage, but my arm swung around and caught Noah under his jaw. He fell to the ground.

Woah!

I was shocked by my reaction. But now, I had the upper hand. Noah was on the floor, and I could tell him exactly how I felt. "He is not retarded; he's gifted, and he is not a liar. Shame on you, Noah Grant. I'd like to tell your mother what kind of a boy you've become, but I won't do that. Unlike you, I still I...you know what, you're an ass."

I spun around and noticed, Kyle and Kevin, sitting in the foyer. They had witnessed the whole encounter between Noah and me. I was mortified; what kind of a girl yells out *ass* in the middle of the church.

I raced out the front door after seeing the two of them and hurried behind the nearest tree to hide. A few minutes went by, and I calmed myself enough to return to the building. I moved away from the backside of the tree and saw Kyle standing a few feet from me.

He smiled awkwardly, then in his muted speech, he asked, "Are you okay?"

"I'm sorry you had to see that, Kyle. I can't believe I caused a scene like that in church." I tried to walk past him, and his hand shot out and caught mine.

"Thank you for ticking up for me."

I'd forgotten how well he read lips. Noah was facing him, and he must have read everything he had said. "Kyle, I'm sorry that you have to put up with narrow-minded people like Noah. I'm done with him; it's time to move on."

"You should have seen his face when he hit the ground. Wow, you have a powerful punch."

I covered my cheeks with my hands. "I can't believe I did that. I wonder how many other people saw me deck him."

Kyle reached forward and pulled one hand off my face. "It was only Kevin and me, but it means a lot to me."

Once again, I couldn't help but think about what incredible eyes he had. "I've got to go back inside; I'm sure my mom's looking for me by now.

"Would you and Kevin like to sit with us for the rest of the meeting?"

"We have to leave early today; my mom is taking us to our gramma's house for a visit. It's a long way from here."

"Oh, I understand." It had been such a long time since he'd spoken to me, let alone carried on a conversation that I was surprised at how sad that made me feel. I hung my head down, not sure what to say or do.

"Can I sit with you next week?"

My head shot up. "I would like that very much, Kyle." I started back toward the church, and he remained by the tree.

I turned around as I remembered something else that I wanted to say now that we were back on speaking terms. "Kyle..." I waited until I had his attention, "If you pass me in the halls at school, please call my name. I don't want to miss seeing you."

He grinned as I raced back into the church just in time to run into Bishop Arnett's chest. "Ruby, why are you always in such a hurry? Slow down. Can I speak to you in my office?"

Oh, boy. "R-right now?"

"I can't think of a better time than right now. It will only take a few minutes."

I followed behind him through the halls trying to find a reasonable explanation for my earlier actions in the church. Someone else besides Kyle and Kevin must have seen me swing at Noah.

We entered his office, and he pointed at one of the open chairs. "Have a seat, Ruby. How are things going at school?"

"Okay, I guess."

"Do you know why I've asked you to come in here?"

"I have a good idea."

"Then I'll get right to it. Mrs. Andrews is the mother of the boy who is deaf in the nursery class you are helping in. She wanted to thank you for doing such a fantastic job with her son, Danny.

"I spoke to Kyle earlier and let him know how much she appreciated his efforts as well. Kyle is a good kid, especially when it comes to handling other special needs kids. I asked him first, and he turned me down. He didn't give me a reason, but I believe he still feels uncomfortable around most adults. I thought I would check with you."

He smiled, pressed his fingertips together, and rested his elbows on the desktop. "I don't know how much you know about sign language, but Kyle said something about you helping one of his teachers at school.

She's the one who teaches sign language, and I thought you might know something since you're her aide?"

"Is that right? I saw him leaving her class a few weeks ago. He must have assumed that was why I was there." I couldn't tell the bishop what I was really doing in her class.

"I'm learning sign language along with her students; I do know quite a few words already."

"You're a bright girl, and that's why I think this opportunity would be great for you. Mrs. Andrews must find a full-time job, it's not something she is happy about, but the needs of her family come first. She has two other children at home who are also deaf, a little girl who is a year younger than Danny and a toddler.

"Mrs. Andrews hates leaving them with just anyone. She could really use the help, and she would pay you. Would you be interested in a job at night watching her three small children? It would be three nights a week."

"When do you need to know, Bishop?" I had to think about what he was asking me to do. I was still trying to learn sign language to surprise Kyle, but the extra money would help at home, and I could buy some things that I wanted.

"By next Sunday, if possible. I asked Kyle last week, and he turned me down today. She wanted someone who could work with her kids. Since you are learning sign language yourself, you would be perfect for the job. Let me know what you decide, Ruby."

I left his office just in time to make my way to the nursery. At least things would be better between Kyle and me now. I entered the room, and his smile when he saw me lit up the space. Then I glanced at Danny Andrews, he was a special boy. I could do so much to help his family if I took the job. But that might take away from my chances to learn sign language quicker.

For the first time in my life, I decided to go home and pray. I didn't know which to choose.

Chapter Six

Babysitting

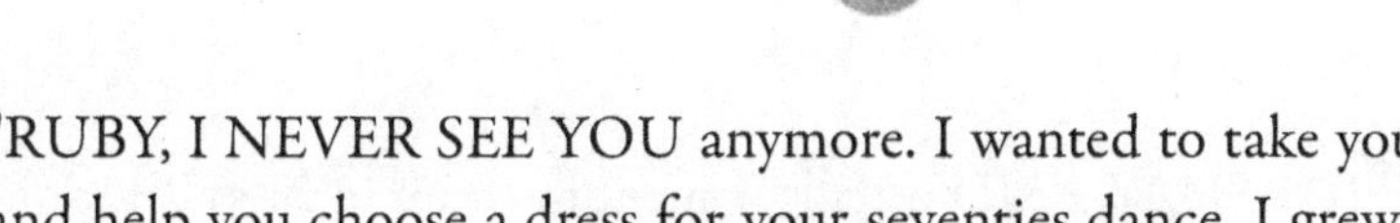

"RUBY, I NEVER SEE YOU anymore. I wanted to take you shopping and help you choose a dress for your seventies dance. I grew up in that era, and I can't wait to help you find something that fits that time period. How many weeks are left before the Disco Ball?"

"Mom, I have so much that I need to do to get ready. Working for Mrs. Andrews is taking all my time, and I still haven't asked Kyle if he'll fix the disco ball. Why, oh why did I volunteer for that job?"

"Which job, my darling. Babysitting, or decorating for the dance?"

"Ugh, both. No, that's not true, I can't wait to decorate, but I don't have time. I've missed a couple of the meetings, and now I might not get to help at all." I was so frustrated with everything.

Mostly myself.

"How are your morning language classes coming? Ruby, you could always give those up."

"No, I can't, Mom. I am not going to stop taking those. Besides, that's one of the reasons Mrs. Andrew hired me. Her kids are adorable, and I am actually doing something worthwhile because I can sign.

"Ruby, I'm off this Saturday; until three in the afternoon. Maybe we could go shopping then. Let me check." Mom pulled out her phone and played with it for a few seconds.

"That works with my schedule. That reminds me, how close are you and Kyle?"

"Wh-what do you mean by that? I see him at school, and we work in the nursery together. Why?"

"Something is going on with his mom, and it has me worried. I don't know how much her kids know, but if you hear anything, will you tell me?"

Now she had me worried. "Sure, Mom. As soon as I see Kyle, I'll ask him."

IT WAS THURSDAY, AND usually, I spent my hour in Miss Branson's class. Then after school, I went straight to Mrs. Andrews's house to babysit. However, she asked if I could work on Saturday afternoon instead.

So tonight, I was able to make the final committee meeting to plan who was doing what. The disco ball sat in my room under the bed, and I hadn't approached Kyle yet to ask him if he could fix it. If I told the committee that it wasn't working yet, they would freak. The success of the dance depended on that stupid ball.

I rushed into Miss Branson's room with my face glued to my phone and ran headfirst into Kyle. "Ouch! Oh, I'm sorry, Kyle. I wanted to ask you a question." Should I use what I've learned from Miss Branson and ask him about the disco ball in sign language? No, I still had an idea of how I wanted that to happen.

He signed and mouthed the words, "What do you want to know?"

"You are so smart about everything. I'm on the committee at school for the seventies dance. They have this old mirror ball that is on a motor. The motor isn't working properly. I told them that I knew someone, meaning you, who might be able to fix it. Do you want to look at it and see if you can...you know, fix it?"

Kyle mouthed the word, "Don't talk so slow; I'm not slow; I'm deaf." Then he kind of smirked and shrugged his shoulders.

"You're a smart ass too," I said that out loud as I started to turn my head.

Kyle tapped me on the shoulder. "I read lips very well. You are pretty when you blush."

I spun around so I wasn't facing him, and put my hands on my cheeks. This conversation was awkward, and I still hadn't gotten the answer to my question.

I turned back toward him and put my hand on his forearm. "Can you fix it or not?" I shrugged my shoulders, put a silly grin on my face, and tipped my head.

"I need to check with my mom. She has been sick."

"Oh, Kyle, I am sorry. I wondered why she wasn't at church last week. Is there anything I can do to help?"

He shrugged. "Maybe. I will ask her when I get home." He turned around and started down the hall, but then he stopped and came back.

"Bring the disco ball to my house tonight. Bye." He left me in a hurry after that.

"Bye Ruby! My name is Ruby, say it, dang it."

I jumped when Miss Branson spoke behind me, "What's the problem, Ruby?"

"Oh my gosh, you scared me. It's no biggy, but...ever since my old boyfriend's pals made fun of the way Kyle said my name, I've never heard him repeat it. To tell you the truth, I kind of egged them on. I was just kidding around, but I haven't heard him say my name since."

"Did he say anything about his mother to you?"

"All I heard was that she wasn't feeling well. I'm going to ask my mom to go with me to their house tonight and see if she needs our help. I thought we could bring a dessert or something else to share. If I find out something, I will let you know."

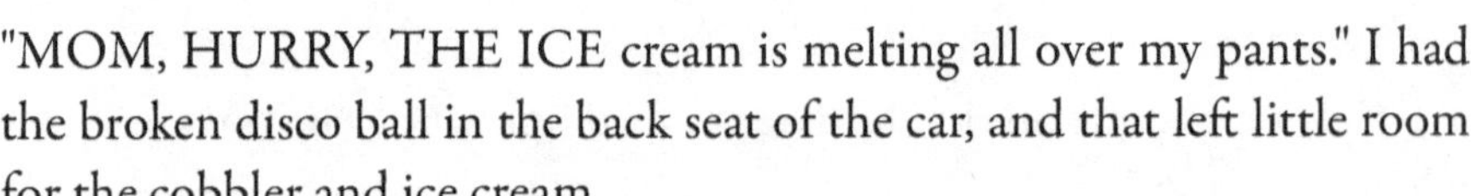

"MOM, HURRY, THE ICE cream is melting all over my pants." I had the broken disco ball in the back seat of the car, and that left little room for the cobbler and ice cream.

"Ruby Lane, hold your horses. I had to get the address from your father. I hope she doesn't mind us showing up like this. I know I'd be unhappy if you invited someone over to our house without asking first."

She squinted at each house, and started mumbling under her breath, "Okay, help me look for their house numbers. I know we were here once before, but I don't remember what it looked like, especially with it being so dark."

"There, it's that one with the old pickup in the driveway. I wonder if we will get to meet their father?"

"I don't know about that, Ruby. Your father said something about him being gone from home all the time. I don't doubt it. The yard could use some work. I'll have your father come over and see if he can get some of the other church members over here to help out."

We waited at the front door for a few minutes before Kevin finally answered the door. "Hey, Mrs. Johnson. Hello Ruby. I don't think my mom was expecting anyone. Can you wait on the porch for just a minute?"

"Sure, Kevin. Is Kyle home, I have something for him in the back seat of my car."

Kevin glanced at the car. "I'll see if I can find him too. Hang on."

The door was closed in our faces, and at any moment the ice cream would start running down my arm. "Mom, maybe we should go back home and call the next time."

"Shush, I think they really could use our help. We'll just wait here for a few more minutes, and then we will ring the..."

The door opened, and Kyle smiled at us. "Kyle, the disco ball is in our car, and the ice cream is melting down my arms."

He didn't know which way to go first. His side-to-side dance was almost comical as he went back and forth from one foot to another. Eventually, reaching for the ice cream was his choice. He took the dessert from my hands and pushed his way into the house. At least the mess now dripped down his arms instead of mine.

"Follow my lead, Ruby." My mother stayed close to his heels.

I whispered as my eyes swept over the room, "Mom, I think something is terribly wrong."

Chapter Seven

Service Project

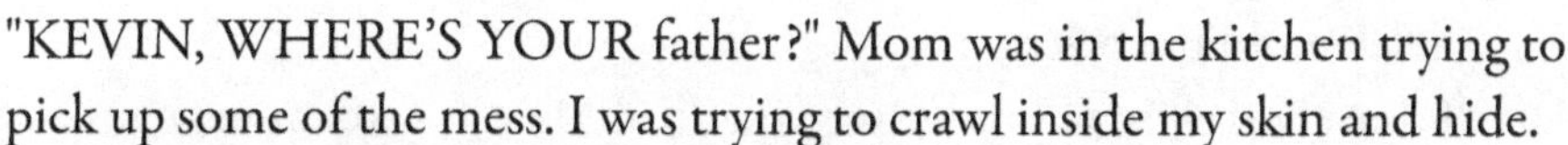

"KEVIN, WHERE'S YOUR father?" Mom was in the kitchen trying to pick up some of the mess. I was trying to crawl inside my skin and hide.

Whose mother does that?

"Mom, maybe it's none of our business. We should go and come back another time."

Kyle's sister came racing into the room and fell on the floor at my feet. She was autistic and non-verbal, and she had been staying home with Mr. Deegan, so his wife could go to church. I hadn't met her yet.

"Kevin, what's your sister's name?"

"Her name is Kelly, and she's supposed to stay in the bedroom with my mom. Kelly, come on. Mom wants you to stay with her and watch television."

My mother spoke up. "Where is your mom, Kevin? I didn't know she was home."

"She's in her bedroom. She's been really sick."

"Kevin, can we go and say hello?"

"Mother, you heard him. She's sick." I tried to grab her arm, but she pushed her way into the woman's bedroom.

"You don't want to catch something." I followed after her and stood in the doorway listening.

"Barbara, what can we do to help you? Your children love you, and I hope you know that we do too." Mom sat down on the corner of the bed.

"I can't believe that you're here. I'm such a mess. I don't know if I can keep going on like this. I love my babies, but it's too much for me to handle every day. Kelly is more than enough by herself. But with Jack gone, I don't know what to do."

"You take it one thing at a time, and I'm here to help. Whatever you do, don't give up.

"I'll speak to the ladies at church if you don't mind, and we can set up a schedule to either take Kelly for the afternoon or we can come in and help cook and clean a few times a week. You tell me what would be more beneficial, and I'll work on it."

"I don't feel right about letting you do all that. It's too much to ask of anyone, Mrs. Johnson."

"We are friends, and I expect you to ask me when you need help. Would you rather things continue the way they are now? I didn't think so.

"The ladies at church are always looking for service projects, and you are very deserving of their time. Please call me Grace."

While they talked, I left the bedroom and went searching for Kyle. I didn't have to go far to find him. He sat in the middle of the kitchen floor with Kelly, and it looked like he was playing a game with her. I stepped back so he wouldn't see me and watched the two of them. The more I saw of Kyle, the harder I fell for him.

He has such a beautiful soul.

Kelly noticed me before Kyle did. She jumped off the floor and tried to hide under the kitchen table.

He turned around and saw me, and once again, his smile lit up the room. "Kelly likes you. She is hiding where she can watch you." He signed as he mouthed the words, and he didn't make a sound.

Since that day at school, when Noah's friends harassed him, I hadn't heard a word from him. "Kyle, does she know how to sign?"

"Yes, she is very smart."

I wanted to show Kyle what I had learned so far from Miss Branson; this would give me the perfect opportunity.

I moved closer to their kitchen table and knelt. I began signing, "Do you want to play, Kelly?"

Kyle tapped me on my shoulder. "She is waiting to see what you are going to play. By the way, she loves her Barbies."

That was good to know, I had a ton of them at home in my bedroom closet. "Kelly, your brother tells me you like Barbies. I have a lot of them at my house. Could I bring them over and play with you?"

She hurried out from under the table and climbed onto my lap. Her exuberance just about knocked me over.

She kept signing, "Play, Kelly, play."

Kyle tapped me again and mouthed. "She likes you."

I wanted to cry. "I like her too." Then I remembered the ice cream and cobbler we'd brought with us to share.

"Kyle, can she have dessert? It's homemade, and we brought enough for two families."

My mother entered the kitchen with Mrs. Deegan following close on her heels. "I think that's a great idea, Ruby. Barbara, where are your plates?"

"MOM, I CAN'T BELIEVE you got her to agree. I promised Kelly I would bring my Barbies over soon and spend some time playing with her. Kyle is going to go help with Mrs. Andrews's kids. We decided to switch it off. I can be at his house when the ladies at church come over with you to help her get organized, and Kyle will earn a little money to help out at home."

"That sounds wonderful, Ruby. I'm very proud of you for volunteering. A child with Asperger's takes lots of love. But if anyone can do it, I know you can."

Now I wondered if I was volunteering for the right reason. Was I doing it to impress her brother, or was I doing it because I cared about the girl? I guess I'd find out next Saturday.

Meanwhile, mom would pass around the signup sheet at church on Sunday and also tell the bishop that Mrs. Deegan needed more help at home. My dad was asking for volunteers at church to help with their yard, and to do the work that was needed inside the house.

"I love you, Mom. The Deegans are a really nice family, and if we hadn't stopped by to check on them, I don't know what would have happened. r once I'm glad you are so persistent. Now I need to find all of my dolls and clean them up to bring them with me on Saturday."

"I've said it many times, Ruby. Persistence and little patience can work miracles."

Chapter Eight

Barbies

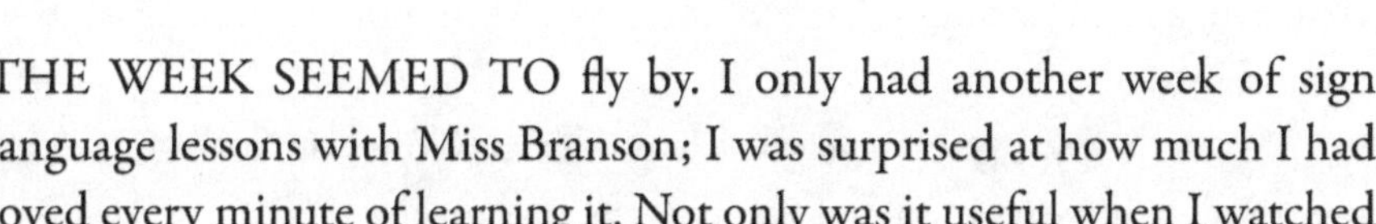

THE WEEK SEEMED TO fly by. I only had another week of sign language lessons with Miss Branson; I was surprised at how much I had loved every minute of learning it. Not only was it useful when I watched Mrs. Andrews's kids, but it would help me communicate with Kelly.

Kyle hadn't been surprised at all when I spoke to Kelly.

That's weird.

Or, maybe he was, and I didn't notice. It didn't matter; I had done something important for myself; I had picked up signing very quickly.

The big dance was next weekend. All week long was spirit week, and I couldn't wait to participate. Kyle was working on repairing the disco ball, and I knew it would be ready in time. The committee was meeting after school today to go over all the assignments.

Becca met me in the hall outside of Miss Branson's classroom. "Can you speak with the deaf, Ruby?"

"Yes, very well in fact. You should take it next semester; it's really fun."

"No, thank you. I'd rather take something fun like shop class if I'm doing it to impress a guy. Don't look so surprised, I've seen you looking at him when he passes you by in the hallways. Why do you even bother? Isn't he sort of...you know, sloowww?" Then she laughed

I stopped and looked at my friend. I was shocked at what she had just said to me. "I can't believe those words came out of your mouth. I guess I don't know you, after all. Becca, what would your mother say if she heard you talk like that?

"Kyle has autism. He is incredibly smart, and he has the sweetest heart. You should see him with his younger sister."

"Is he fixing the disco ball? Right now, that's all I'm worried about. You do know that the whole dance theme is centered around that working."

"Yes, he's fixing it. I guess he's not so slow after all, is he?" It seemed that everyone I thought I once knew wasn't as understanding as they should be.

"Sorry, Ruby. I guess I've got a lot to learn. Come on, let's get to that meeting, or it won't matter if we have the ball or not."

WE ALL GOT OUR ASSIGNMENTS for the following Saturday. Becca and I were working on the decorations, along with a few of the other girls. Noah and his friend Greg were on the decorating committee.

He grinned at me as the group members were assigned. "Don't look at me, Noah Smith. It's just a committee; we aren't dating again."

"Give me another chance, Ruby. If you do, I'm pretty sure that I'll get you to change your mind about me."

Kyle's soft eyes flashed through my mind. "Never in a million years. I've got more important things to do and to think about besides you."

"Yea? Well I don't believe that. I guess we will see what happens. I'll see you next Saturday, Ruby."

Jerk.

I waited until he walked away and then growled. "Grrr, I don't like him at all anymore. I wish he were in another group."

Becca's smirk irritated me. "The lady doth protest too much. I'll bet you dance with him more than once at the Disco Ball."

"Oh, yea? What do you want to bet? I won't set foot anywhere near him again if I can help it. He's not the same kid I first met; he's changed a lot since he started high school."

"We all have, Ruby. It's called growing up. Like I said, you doth protest too much."

I SHOWED UP AT THE Deegan's house with my mom and my dad on Saturday morning. I'd gone through all my Barbies, and I'd thrown away a lot of things, but I still had an awesome assortment of dolls to give to her.

"Ruby, that's a very sweet thing for you to do. I know how much your collection meant to you."

"They still do, Mom, but Kelly will appreciate them more than I will now. I will admit that I played with them secretly in my room last night. I'm sure I can come over anytime and play Barbies with her here."

Kevin answered the door. "Come inside. The bishop is already here with Mr. Evans and the relief society president."

Kevin noticed me, and what I had in my arms, and grinned. "I know who those are for. Kelly is waiting for you in her bedroom."

"Did Kyle leave already? I was hoping to talk to him a little bit about Danny before he went over there. I guess he'll figure it out on his own.

"Kelly, here I come." I planned to stay with her in her room for most of the day. There would be a lot of strange people in the house, and I knew how upsetting it would be to her. If I kept her focused on the Barbies, I felt she would be okay. I'd also brought snacks for us to share.

I followed Kevin down the hall to Kelly's room. He opened her bedroom door, and I followed him inside. As soon as he opened the door, she was dressed and waiting for me.

She pounced on me. "Kelly, look what I brought for us." I turned to face Kevin, "Will she mind being in here with the door closed?"

"Nope, she prefers the quiet, and the door closed. You being in here with her will help her stay calm. And it will keep her out of trouble. Huh, Kelly Boo?"

"Kevin, will you let me know how things are going with the house. I don't want Kelly to get upset while everyone is here."

"Sure. My mom wants me to show the men who show up what needs to be done the most in the yard and the house. Then I can come in here and play with both of you if you want me to."

"Thanks, Kevin. I think we'd both like that."

I closed her door and took out each of my dolls, and introduced them to Kelly. This was great practice for my signing skills, and in a way, it helped me say goodbye to my childhood playmates. I'd logged in a ton of hours with my dolls, and hadn't realized until that moment how difficult this would be for me.

This is a good cause.

MY AFTERNOON FLEW BY with Kelly and Kevin. There had been only one time when the lawnmower was running right outside of her window. She panicked and covered her ears, but Kevin helped her calm down. After that incident, we were good again.

There was a knock at the door. I assumed it was my mom or one of the other ladies from the church. "Come in."

Kyle opened the door and grinned, "Kelly, did you have a good day with your new friend?" He did it again.

Or didn't.

He wouldn't say my name. Now I was beginning to think it was on purpose. "We had a great time, Kyle. How was your day with Danny? I wanted to warn you about his biting but forgot."

He held his finger. "I found out on my own."

"I'm sorry. Ouch, that looks sore." I hoped to spend more time with him, but he stood quietly inside the room.

I guess that's my clue to go.

"Kelly, can I come and play with you again next week?"

She clung to me as Kyle answered for her. "She doesn't want you to go now. I will have my mom come and get her so that you can leave. Shall I tell her you will be here next Saturday?"

"Absolutely. I will see you then too. Mrs. Andrews has next week off and doesn't need me until the week after that. Bye, Kyle."

I went looking for my parents, and turned to see Kyle waving at me from the door. For some reason that gave me hope. I grinned stupidly as I waved back.

It's not over yet.

Chapter Nine

Spirit Week

IT WAS SPIRIT WEEK, and I was stoked; I loved doing crazy things. The week would be a blur full of fun activities at school. I had the list tacked on my bulletin board in my bedroom, and I had already planned each day out carefully.

Today, I wore my red sweater and blue jeans, which I rolled up at the bottom as my mom showed me to do. I had on my white tennis shoes and red ankle socks. I put my hair in pigtails and wore huge white bows over the elastics.

I hurried into Miss Branson's classroom. "I'm so excited for this week. When are you going to test me?"

"What are you doing Thursday after school?"

I had to move my brain forward a few days. "Tuesday is hair day, Wednesday's backward day, and Thursday is...It's PJ day, I don't have anything else going on until Friday. Saturday I'll be decorating for the dance."

"Then I can test you Thursday afternoon. Ruby, you are a pleasure to work with. I hope you use your talents when you leave school. Many places can use a friendly person who signs well. I'll go over everything with you this week, and if you can think of anything else that you want to learn, let me know."

THE REST OF THE DAY was a blast. We had an assembly during the first part of the day, and the teachers put on a skit where they acted like they were at a dance in the seventies. The music was cool, and I already loved the Bee Gees. I sang every word with them during the skit.

I passed Kyle in the hallway at lunchtime, and he just waved at me. He seemed to be in a hurry, or I might have approached him. I still wanted to hear him say my name.

In Mr. Christiansen's class, we had a sub who didn't care what we did, so Deborah and I talked about what we were wearing at the Disco Ball.

"Did Kyle get the ball working yet?"

"Oh, crap. I forgot to ask him about it. I hoped he would get it to me before Saturday. I'm supposed to meet with the others around noon to start decorating. We will need the ball then. Maybe I'll see him leaving Miss Branson's room, but only if get there immediately after the bell."

I WAS ABLE TO TALK my way into getting excused from the last part of the seventh period and hurried over to Miss Branson's room. She was still teaching, so I waited outside of her door. I was anxious to speak to Kyle.

I had something to ask him about besides the disco ball. I'd turned down a few offers to go to the dance with other boys in school, but I wanted to ask Kyle if he would go with me first. I planned on doing it all in sign language. He knew I could sign already, but I had practiced my invitation over and over again to make it perfect and unique.

Finally, there was no one left inside her classroom but Kyle. "Hey, Miss Branson, can I borrow Kyle for just a minute?"

"Sure, Ruby. But why don't you ask him yourself?"

Okay, here goes nothing. I grabbed Kyle's hand and led him down the hall after me to a private nook so that we wouldn't be disturbed. I was nervous, but I'd been working on this for weeks.

You got this.

I began my signing. "Kyle Deegan. I love your wit I love your style. You make me laugh; you make me smile. Please do me the honor of being my date for the Disco Ball; I can hardly wait." He watched me without moving a muscle, and fleetingly I thought, he probably doesn't know I'm rhyming.

I continued. "It's retro Saturday the nights all a twitter, but it won't be unless you come dressed in your best glitter. Kyle, will you be my date for the Disco Ball on Saturday night? I want you to be my first dance partner."

He continued to gawk at me. "Kyle?" My hands were sweating, I'd never asked a boy out on a date before. We hadn't been there too long, but suddenly I felt awkward and confused.

Did I speak to fast?

He smiled, shrugged his shoulders, and turned around and walked down the hall.

"Kyle? Why do you do always do this to me?"

Don't you dare cry.

But I couldn't help it. I ran out of the school, and hid behind a large tree so no one would see me crying like a baby.

THAT AFTERNOON WHEN I got home from school, the disco ball was sitting in a box on my front porch with a handwritten note attached to the side of the box. 'It works.'

If I hadn't been so excited to see the shiny object, I would have screamed out my frustrations. "Kyle Deegan, why don't you like me?"

I picked up the box and carried it into my room. I lifted it out of the box and plugged it in. Sure enough, the thing spun in my hand as if it were brand new.

"Dang it, Kyle. What can I do to get you to notice me?" I had no clue at this point. I'd done everything I could to get him to acknowledge me.

You're not his type.

But I could be his type. His brother Kevin might have some ideas, or his mother even. I wasn't ready to give up, not yet.

THE REST OF THE WEEK went well. I searched the halls for a glimpse of my disco hero, and I didn't see him not even once during the entire week.

When I walked into the house on Wednesday night, my mother was there waiting for me. She was anxious to take me to get shoes and she'd made an appointment to get my nails done and my hair cut.

My mother was smart, and she was the only hope I had.

At least for now.

"Mom?" We were in the car and headed to the mall.

"Ruby Lane?"

"Can I ask you a personal question?"

"That sounds serious, should I be afraid?"

"When did you know that you liked, Dad?"

"Oh, it is serious. Do you mean like, like, or love like?"

"I don't know."

"Is this about, Kyle Deegan?"

I turned in my seat to look at her. "How did you know that?"

She giggled as she peeked at me. "I'm your mother, and mothers know everything about their children. I saw you looking at him the night we were at their home. He is a nice boy, and very attentive to his little sister also. Does he like you back?"

"I don't know, but I wished that he did. He's nothing like any other boy I've ever liked. He is kind, and he treats his little sister like she is a normal girl. But..."

"You want him to notice you. I was a girl once too. Your father was a jock, and he could have had any girl in high school that he wanted, but he was holding out for me. I thought he was cute, but I didn't pay him any mind until he began ignoring me. That was all it took, and after that, we were inseparable."

"I don't think that would work with Kyle. He'd probably notice me more if I had a handicap."

"Ruby, what an insensitive thing to say."

"Yea, I know. But it's true. He's so good to his sister, and he helps Miss Branson in class with her students every day as well. Mom, it's almost like he doesn't know I exist, and he won't even say my name out loud anymore. Perhaps I should apologize to him for what happened a few weeks ago. Maybe then he would listen to me."

"Ruby Lane, you had better start talking from the beginning and don't leave a single thing out."

So, I did as she asked, and spilled the beans; every one of them. I told her what happened in the halls at school with Noah and his friends, and then I explained that the reason why I took the signing classes in the first place was to impress Kyle. I even blurted out my reasons for being kind to his sister. It was so he would notice me more. But even that backfired when I really started to care for her after spending time with her on Saturday.

Then I told her about my feeble attempt to ask him to the disco ball dance. "Mom, he didn't say a thing, but turned around and left me standing in the hall."

"Ruby, you do have an apology to make. How could you let it go this long? I told you Noah Smith was up to no good.

"After we go shopping, you should go over to Kyle's house and talk to him in person. Explain what happened at school and tell him what amends you have done to make up for your hurtful behavior toward him. I hope he can forgive you enough to consider going with you to the dance on Saturday night but don't hold your breath."

We turned into the mall parking lot, and Mom started up and down the lanes looking for the closest spot.

"On the other hand, I'm proud of you for working so hard to learn sign language. You can get an excellent job with that skill. When do you take your final exam?"

"Tomorrow. Maybe I could use that as an excuse to get Kyle to talk to me; I could tell him I need help to pass the test."

"Or you could be truthful and tell him you are sorry for what happened a few weeks ago and ask him if he would mind helping you study, not that you deserve his help. Ruby, life is hard the first time around. Learn from your mistakes and grow because of them, and not in spite of them."

"I love you, Mom. How did you get so smart?"

"Maybe it's because I had a brilliant mother. Come on, Ruby," She pulled into the first slot next to the door and turned off the car.

"We're here. Let's find you the perfect pair of disco shoes. If we find them quick enough, we might have time for some ice cream."

Chapter Ten

Disco Ball

I EASILY PASSED MY test with Miss Branson, and she gave me a certificate to prove it. I couldn't wait to show my mom when I got home.

"Good for you, Ruby. Did you hear back from Kyle yet?"

"No," and I didn't see him at all today. However, I was going to the dance no matter what. I did hope that he would change his mind and come with me, even knowing how much hurt my actions might have caused.

"After I apologized to him Wednesday night, he nodded and thanked me for coming over. Then he told me he would see me at school."

I reached for my mom's hand, and as I took it, I sniffled to hold back the flood of emotions I felt might hit me at any moment.

"Thank you for loving me no matter what, Mom."

"It's okay, Ruby." She put her arms around me, and we stayed that way for some time. "I'll always love you no matter what you do, sweet girl."

FRIDAY ARRIVED, AND it was the end of spirit week. We had another assembly, and this time, the drama class put on a satire performance of 'Staying Alive'. It was silly and made the rest of the day fun, and it flew by quickly for me.

Tomorrow's the big night.

I met my friends at school to start decorating. I had the disco ball with me, and Noah and his buddy Greg got on the ladder and hung it from the hook in the middle of the room. We had most of the decorations up by then, and when the ball spun around, it sent shards of light spinning throughout the room.

The patterns it made on the walls mesmerized me. "Kyle, I wish you could be here and see this." But that wasn't going to happen. I'd never heard back from him, nor had I seen him at all in school.

Dang.

The room was all finished, and it was time for me to go home and get dressed for the dance.

I LOOKED AT MY REFLECTION in the glass. I didn't look like the same girl who had started high school. I had matured both physically and mentally. High school would be over in a few short months, and I wasn't sure if I was ready for it to end.

Big hair was in during the seventies, and tonight I wore mine curled and wavy. I had a red silk scarf around my neck that matched my shoes. My dress was form-fitting on top and flared out just below my knees.

My mom did my makeup, and it was dramatic and different. I looked like a grown-up and wanted to turn around and go back to the way things were a few years ago. I wasn't entirely ready to give up my childhood, and yet I was more than eager for the next chapter in my life to begin.

I'd never heard back from Kyle, but I didn't accept anyone else's offer to go to the dance either. Deborah and I were going to show up together and see what happened. We could spend the night dancing with each other, and we were okay with it. But since we were also part of the decorating committee, we each had to take a turn to welcome the students as they arrived, and then direct them to the different areas in the auditorium.

Noah was on the opposite side of the door from me, and he continued to flirt. "Noah, I'm just not into you anymore. I'm sorry. Truly, I am."

"Can we have just one dance together, Ruby? Please, for old times' sake."

"Do you know how corny that sounds, Noah?"

"Yes, I do; just tell me if it worked."

"Okay, but just the one time. Don't ask me again."

"I tried texting you earlier to ask you again. Didn't you get my messages?"

"That's silly. We were in the same auditorium together, and no, I left my phone home. But my answer would have been the same then as it is now." In some ways, I wished Noah hadn't shown me his true colors.

Did I really?

"You know what? I'm tired of hearing you whine. Come on, let's get this over with." I took Noah's hand, and he led me to the dance floor.

It figured that the song that came on next was a slow one. "Noah, can we skip this one?"

"Nope. You promised me a dance, and I'm choosing this one. Hang on and enjoy the ride."

"Wow, just how corny can you get?"

"You ain't seen nothing yet." He laughed, and then gathered me close. It was almost like old times.

Almost.

"Hmmm. You smell really good, Ruby."

"Don't get used to it. This is the last chance dance."

He pulled back and considered my eyes. "That sounds like an offer. I'll take it."

"It wasn't meant that way; I'm just saying this is our last dance."

The dance ended, and I tried to pull away. "One more, Ruby. Please?"

"No. I've got to find Deborah." I pulled free of his hand and started toward the door that led outside.

Is that Kyle.

I swear it was him watching us from the doorway? "Kyle?" I yelled his name as I ran toward him.

He looked disheveled and scared. He spoke and signed the words he needed to tell me, but he was frantic and ran his words together. However, now I understood what he was saying.

"I need your help, please. Kelly is missing."

"Oh, my God! How long has she been gone, Kyle?"

"We need to find her." He took my hand and tried to pull me outside the door.

"Kyle, tell me what happened. Stop. Look at me. What happened to Kelly, and how long has she been missing?" I signed as I mouthed the words.

He looked more than scared now. He also looked angry and hurt. "You told her last week that you would be back this Saturday and play dolls with her. She waited for you for hours."

"What? I didn't...Oh crap. I did tell her that. I made her that promise before I remembered I was decorating for the dance. God, I'm sorry. How long has she been gone, and where do you think she went?"

Kyle was noticeably upset, but he spoke as slowly as he could. "Kelly remembered seeing me working on that disco ball. I told her I was making it for you. I also told her it would be at a party at the school, and I wanted to bring her here to see it.

"That's why I didn't tell you yes when you asked me to the dance. I wanted to bring Kelly and hoped we could all dance together. But then I went to get her, and she was gone."

"Kyle, does she know where the school is?"

"Yes, she comes with my mom every morning to take Kevin and me both to school."

"She could be on her way here now. Did your mom call the police?"

"Yes, and she tried to call you, but you didn't answer your phone." He was visibly shaking.

"Kyle, look at me. We will find her; I will help you look for her. Come on." We left the school grounds together, it was dark, and she could be hiding anywhere.

"Kyle, how does your mom usually drive to school? We can backtrack and call her name while we are looking."

We continued down the streets calling Kelly's name. "Stop...Kyle, did you hear that?" I grabbed his arm.

I heard the distinct sound of someone calling my name. "Kelly, I hear you. Call my name, louder."

Kyle couldn't hear her.

But I did.

"I can't believe how clearly she says my name. I wish you could hear her. There she is. Look, Kyle, Kelly's by that fence next to the rose bushes."

I heard her call out my name again, and it was clear as could be. "Ruby, I miss you, Ruby."

I threw my arms around her, and Kyle circled her from the other side.

Kelly was safe.

I pointed in the direction of the Deegan's home. "Look, Kyle. There's the police. You stay here with her, and I will flag them down."

The police stopped in front of Kelly and Kyle, and shortly after they arrived, his mother came with my mom driving her.

"Kelly, are you okay? My darling girl, I thought I'd lost you for good."

"Mrs. Deegan, she is safe, and she looks great. Kyle and I found her. It appears as if she was on the way to the dance to find me. I'm sorry I didn't show up at your house today. She went out on her own, and it was all my fault."

My mom admonished me. "You need to remember your promises, Ruby Lane. Sometimes the superficial things don't mean as much when you put the rest of life in perspective. Once the police officers take Mrs.

Deegan's statement and make sure Kelly is all right. I'll take them both home."

My mother looked at Kyle, and then at me. "Ruby, are you going back to the dance?"

I glanced at Kyle, he was still clinging to his sister. "I'm not sure. I need to question Kyle about his sister. We need to make a joint plan for her. I'll give you a call if I need a ride home. I love you, Mom."

"Love you too, Ruby. That boy's a keeper. I hope things work out the way you would like them to."

I waited until all the vehicles had left us, and then turned to look for Kyle. He was standing right behind me.

A chill coursed through my body when I saw him walking toward me. "Hey Kyle, I was wondering how Kelly learned to say my name so well?"

Kyle watched the rest of the taillights until they were out of sight before he moved closer to me. "I taught her how to say your name. Miss Branson was helping me learn to say my Rs so I could surprise you."

"Really? Kyle, I want to hear you say it." I had waited for six weeks to hear him say my name, and I wasn't going to wait any longer.

"Kyle, say my name!"

"Ruby."

"Thank you, Kyle." It was one simple word, but it meant the world to me.

"Wait. You didn't let me finish. Ruby, I would love to go to the Disco Ball Dance with you."

Epilogue

Ruby

I TOOK KYLE'S HAND and led him into the ballroom. I pointed at the ball above our heads. "You know this wouldn't be happening if it weren't for your efforts. You are so talented."

"I know." He shrugged.

"You do, do you?" I had to giggle. "Thank you, Kyle."

"Ruby, I never danced before."

"Really? So this is your first time? Watch me, and do whatever I do. Wait, you can't hear the music."

"But I can feel it."

"Then why don't I follow you. Come on it's easy." I moved my feet back and forth and then started swinging my arms at the same time.

Kyle was hesitant at first, but eventually, he caught on.

He is so awesome.

I never had so much fun as I did at that dance.

"Kyle," I was supposed to help with the cleanup when it was over, but I wasn't ready for Kyle to go yet. "I want to walk home with you, but I have to stay..." He looked around the room, and before I said another word, Kyle started picking up the empty cups and other garbage off the floor.

"Wow, my mom was right. You're a keeper."

ONCE EVERYTHING WAS back in its place. Deborah found me and Kyle. "Ruby, do you need a ride home. My mom's already outside waiting for me"

I peeked at Kyle. "No thanks, but can I borrow your phone before you leave?"

"Sure. Hey Ruby, is this Kyle?" I introduced them and while they tried to talk to one another, I called my mother.

"Mom, I know it's late, but is it all right if I walk with Kyle back to his house? It's a beautiful night, and his house isn't that far, and..."

"Ruby Lane. Stop your chatter and let me talk. First of all, did you have a nice time?"

"It was amazing. I think we danced to every song. Kyle's a better dancer than I am. So, can I walk with him?"

"Yes, but no dawdling, and don't you linger too long once you get there. I know tomorrow is Saturday, but I don't want your father to have to wait up too long for us to go to bed. You know how he gets at night."

"Thanks, Mom."

"You're welcome, Ruby."

...THAT NIGHT WAS THE first of many nights together. It was true, Kyle was a much better dancer than I was, and once we were married, he took me dancing every chance he could.

I sure do miss him, and those incredible eyes of his. He died of liver cancer a few years back, but I'll never forget the last words he spoke before he passed away in my arms...

"Ruby, once you get to heaven, I expect you to save the first dance for me."

"Kyle, You're the first and only one I'll ever dance with in heaven. I love You, Kyle."

"I love, you. Ruby..." My name was the last thing I heard him say.

About The Author:

Robin Rance is married but spent twenty-two years as a single mother of five before she married her forever husband. She was a letter carrier for twenty-four years and is now retired from the postal service. Now she lives in Southern Utah, where she writes, cooks, and spends quality time with her family and grandkids.

Robin began writing after a reoccurring dream kept making an appearance. She wakes up regularly with other stories begging to be told. Robin generally writes contemporary romance but has also written other genres, including inspirational romance, fantasy, historical fiction, and three children's books.

Did you love *Call My Name*? Then you should read *Worth The Fight*[1] by Robin Rance and Robin Rance!

[2]

Worth The Fight

Ally

Did he just call me fat? As soon as he took off for the garage, I twirled around in front of the big picture mirror that covered the south wall of the living room. As a young girl, I had always hated this mirror, and after seeing all my imperfections, now, I hated it even more.

I sat down on the oversized, outdated couch, picked up the remote, and switched on the TV. The only thing that would make me feel better, besides food, was to lose myself in one of my favorite episodes of Outlander.

---

1. https://books2read.com/u/mgjL27

2. https://books2read.com/u/mgjL27

"Jamie, Jamie, Jamie. You wouldn't care that I might have grown too big for my breeks, now, would ya?" If I didn't have the excitement Jamie brought to my life, I don't know what I would do.

Brock

I loved Ally, more than life itself, but I couldn't take her rejection anymore. We no longer seemed to have the same interests. We had so much fun together when we first met. When did everything change?

She'd put on a few pounds, but who didn't as they aged. Okay, I hadn't. I was a freak of nature, and Al resented me for it. So, instead of listening to her grumbling about it, I set up a gym in the garage, hoping she would use it with me. But, whenever I ask her to join me, she throws it back in my face and refuses.

We hadn't been married that long, and I wanted the closeness we used to have, I wanted my wife back. But sadly, I believe she's fallen for someone else. I've heard her whisper the name Jamie in her sleep.

I don't know who he is, but when I find out...

Also by Robin Rance

Blood Red

Blood Red

Blood Red II, The Curse

Brides Of Benson

Buttercup Price

Dead In The Dust

Ruby's Heartache

Consequences

The Affair

Fireball

Oh Merci

Comfortably Numb

Love On The Rocks

Just One Kiss

It Started With A Kiss

Street Life

Street Secret

Street Hustle

Standalone

Aries Jones

Listen

Looking For Mr. Right

Graysen Cooper

About Jack

Turn The Page

Call My Name

The Promise Of Spring

I'm Dreaming Of Christmas

Worth The Fight

A Fae's Magik

Saving Aurora

Street Savvy

Icy Fingers

Mr. Candy Cain

www.ingramcontent.com/pod-product-compliance
Lightning Source LLC
LaVergne TN
LVHW041237150826
845673LV00008B/2404

* 9 7 9 8 2 3 0 4 7 8 5 2 2 *